Skipper and Sky

Sky blinked. She could see the deep blue sea stretching off into the distance.

"Isn't it amazing?" Skipper woofed, his tail wagging madly.

Sky pressed her pink nose against the window. She looked out at the endless, shining waves. "Oh, I really wish I could go out to sea!" she mewed softly.

Skipper stopped wagging his tail. Had Sky said that she wanted to go out to sea? No, he must have heard that wrong. Cats didn't like water!

Skipper and Sky

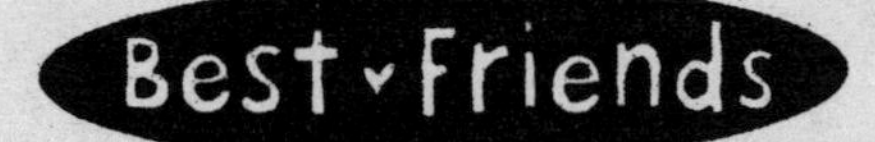

Skipper and Sky

by Jenny Dale
Illustrated by Susan Hellard

SCHOLASTIC INC.

NEW YORK TORONTO LONDON AUCKLAND SYDNEY
MEXICO CITY NEW DELHI HONG KONG BUENOS AIRES

ISBN 0-439-79119-7

12 11 10 9 8 7 6 5 4 3 5 6 7 8 9 10/0

Printed in the U.S.A.
First printing, October 2005

Special thanks to Narinder Dhami

chapter one

"I wish I could go out to sea!" Sky mewed. The silver tabby kitten sat down on the harbor wall and flicked her tail from side to side. Big green waves splashed against the wall below her. Drops of white spray clung to her whiskers, making her fur tingle.

Sky loved the sea. She lived with her owner, Joe, and his family in a cottage next to the harbor. More than anything else, Sky wanted to go out of the harbor on a boat, and across the sea.

She looked at the fishing boats bobbing up and down on the sparkling water. The fishermen were getting ready to leave. Sky could see Joe on the long wooden jetty that stood on legs above the sea at one side of the harbor. He was helping his father fold up the nets. Joe's dad was a fisherman, and his boat was named the *Jolly Jack.*

Joe's dad is so lucky, thought Sky. *He can go out in his boat whenever he wants!*

"Hello, Sky." Joe caught sight of her and waved.

Sky blinked her special cat greeting and jumped down from the harbor wall. As she padded over to see him, she lifted her pink nose and sniffed the salty air. It was early in the day, but the sun already felt warm on Sky's thick fur. Sky purred loudly, thinking of all the tasty fish Joe's dad would catch today. "This is the best place to live in the whole world!" she mewed happily.

Sky sat down and sniffed the air again. She could smell something new. She turned around to see what it was.

A man and a puppy were walking along the path to the harbor. The man had a round, friendly face and a gray beard. The puppy's coat was dark brown and very scruffy, and he had big brown eyes.

Joe's dad waved at the man. "Hello, Mac," he called. "Hello, Skipper."

"Hello, Mr. Kirby," called Mac. "Lovely

day today, isn't it? I wish I was going out on the boat with you!"

Joe's dad smiled. "You haven't met my son yet, have you?" he asked. "Joe, this is Mac, the new lighthouse keeper."

Sky jumped up as Joe went over to meet Mac. She wanted to say hello, too!

The puppy watched, his dark eyes bright and eager, as Sky padded over. "Hello," he woofed, wagging his tail. "I'm Skipper. I live in the lighthouse."

"Hello," Sky mewed. "I'm Sky." She stretched her neck to stare at the tall red-and-white tower on the cliff beyond the little harbor. She had never been to the lighthouse, but she had always been curious about the enormous tower. Sky knew that it had a big light that flashed on

and off when it was dark or foggy. But she didn't know what the light was for. "Do you really live *there*?" she asked.

"Oh, yes," Skipper barked. "Looking after the lighthouse is a very important job!"

Sky opened her eyes wide. She liked Skipper. The puppy was very friendly — his tail never stopped wagging! She was just about to ask him what the lighthouse was for, when Mac called to his puppy.

"Come on, Skipper," he said. "Let's go and get that lightbulb."

"OK, Mac," Skipper woofed. He turned to Sky. "We're picking up a new bulb for the lighthouse," he explained.

"Maybe I'll see you later," Sky mewed. She watched as Skipper followed Mac to the post office on the other side of the harbor.

"Sky?" Joe's dad called from the boat. "Look what I've found!" He held up a plump, silver fish.

Sky purred and scampered down the jetty toward the boat. The wood felt smooth and warm under her paws. Mr. Kirby threw the fish to her, and Sky neatly caught it. Then she ran off and hid behind some crab pots to eat it.

"Yum!" she mumbled through a mouthful of tasty fish. When she had finished, she washed herself from her ears to the tip of her tail. *That's my favorite breakfast*, she thought. *My favorite lunch and dinner, too!*

The fishing boats were ready to leave. Sky padded out from behind the crab pots and stared out to sea. Sunshine sparkled on the water, and the waves were tipped with white foam. Sky couldn't imagine anything better than being in a boat on a day like today, bobbing up and down on the shimmering sea.

She looked around. Mr. Kirby and Joe were talking to one of the other fishermen. This was her chance! Her heart thumping with excitement, Sky padded over to the *Jolly Jack* and jumped on board.

She hunted around for a good place to sit. On the other side of the deck there was a pile of fishy-smelling nets that looked very comfy. Sky climbed on top of

them, sat down, and tucked her paws underneath her. She began to purr loudly, imagining the adventure ahead of her. The boat would skim over the waves in the warm sun. There would be a cool, salty breeze as they sped along. The nets would be thrown into the water, and would soon be full of silver fish. Sky purred even louder. She would be able to eat as many fish as she liked!

Suddenly, two big hands grabbed her around her furry tummy and lifted her into the air. Sky yowled angrily.

"Look what I've found," Joe's dad laughed.

"Put me down!" the kitten mewed, wriggling. "I'm going out to sea!"

"Has she tried to come on board

again?" laughed one of the other fishermen. "She hid in that empty crab pot last time, remember?"

"Sky, don't you know that cats are supposed to hate water?" Joe sighed. He came over to take the kitten from his dad, and rubbed his cheek on the top of her head. "Why do you keep trying to get on Dad's boat?"

"Because I want to go out to sea," Sky mewed, peering over Joe's shoulder as he carried her back down the jetty. She watched sadly as the fishing boats chugged out of the harbor. Why *couldn't* she go with them? It wasn't fair!

chapter two

"Come on, Mac," Skipper barked. He trotted out of the post office, his tail wagging madly. He was very excited because Mac had just received a new bulb for the lighthouse. The bulb was very big, and it was packed in a huge cardboard box.

"Don't get under my feet, Skipper," Mac panted, as he carried the box out of the post office.

"I won't," Skipper woofed. "Just make sure you don't drop the lightbulb!"

They began to walk back to the parking lot. Skipper watched Mac the entire time to make sure he didn't trip over anything.

Skipper looked around the harbor.

Most of the fishing boats had left, and Joe had, too. So had the kitten that had been sitting on the wall. Skipper was disappointed. Sky had seemed very friendly.

"Good morning," Mac said to a man selling ice cream. He put the box down on the ground and stopped to chat.

Skipper began to sniff his way down the wooden jetty. It was full of interesting smells. A fisherman was mending a net at the far end of the jetty. Skipper thought about saying hello, but the fisherman looked a little grumpy. So the puppy kept away from him.

There was another net on the ground. Skipper sniffed his way over to it.

"Are you coming, Skipper?" Mac called from the end of the jetty. He had picked up the box and was ready to go.

Skipper was about to run back to his owner when he stopped. What was that? There was something moving in the net! He padded over to take a closer look.

"I'll see you back at home, Skipper," Mac called, and got in the car to drive back with the lightbulb. He knew that Skipper loved to run home across the cliffs to the lighthouse — it wasn't far.

Skipper prodded the net with his paw.

It was rolled up in a big heap, and he couldn't see what was inside. He hoped the moving thing wasn't a crab. They had very sharp, snappy claws.

He pushed his nose into the net and sniffed. "Who's there?" he woofed. It didn't smell like a fish at all. It smelled like a cat!

"HELP!" Sky yowled. She was very upset. She had been trying to reach a tasty piece of fish in the middle of the net, when the net had wrapped itself around her legs and her tail. She had tried to pull herself free, but the more Sky struggled, the more she got tangled up. The net had wrapped around her tighter and tighter. Now she was really stuck.

Skipper pushed at the net with his nose.

"Is that you, Sky?" he barked. He could just see the kitten's tail twitching. "It's me, Skipper."

"I'm stuck!" Sky wailed. She wriggled around until she could turn her head and look up at the puppy. "Please help me!"

"Of course I will," Skipper woofed. He tried to pull the net away with his paw, but

it was too heavy. Then he had another idea. "Keep still," he told Sky.

Skipper bent his head and began to bite one corner of the net. If he could chew a small hole, then the kitten could squeeze out. The net wasn't easy to break, but Skipper's teeth were strong.

Sky watched the puppy chewing away at the net. Her heart was thumping. What would she do if Skipper couldn't get her out? But soon, Skipper had made a tiny hole in the net. The hole grew bigger and bigger. Sky felt the net beginning to loosen around her.

"Try now," Skipper woofed.

Sky began to squeeze through the hole. It was a very tight fit. She puffed and panted as she pushed herself through.

The net tugged at her fur, and it felt like she was going to get tangled up again. But at last she squeezed out of the hole, and landed on the jetty next to Skipper's paws.

"Are you all right?" Skipper asked, giving her a gentle nudge with his nose.

"Yes, I'm fine," Sky purred. "Thank you for helping me."

"That's OK," Skipper woofed. He looked down at Sky, who was busy grooming her ruffled fur. Skipper hadn't made any friends yet because he and Mac had only moved into the lighthouse a few days ago. Maybe Sky could be his very first friend!

Just then they heard an angry shout from behind them.

"Hey! What have you done to my net?"

Sky and Skipper spun around. The grumpy fisherman was running toward them. He looked even grumpier now!

"Quick!" Skipper woofed. "Let's get out of here!"

The kitten and the puppy raced off down the jetty. The fisherman chased after them, puffing and panting. "Leave my nets alone!" he yelled.

Skipper raced along the path that led from the harbor toward the lighthouse. Sky followed him, running as fast as she could. They ran all the way across the cliff path and didn't stop until they got to the lighthouse. Then they looked back to see if the fisherman was still chasing them. He was nowhere to be seen.

"I think we're safe!" Sky puffed. She

turned and stared up at the red-and-white tower looming over them. She had to crane her neck to see the top. "I've never been all the way to the lighthouse before," she mewed in a small voice. "It's *enormous*!"

Skipper wagged his tail hard. "It's great, isn't it?" he woofed. "Why don't you come inside and have a look around?"

chapter three

Skipper trotted up some stone steps and through the front door of the lighthouse. Sky followed him inside, then stopped in her tracks. There was a spiral staircase in front of her. The stairs seemed to go on forever! Around and around and around, higher and higher and higher.

"Come on," called Skipper.

Sky looked around curiously as she followed. The bottom part of the lighthouse was where Skipper and Mac lived. There was a kitchen, a bedroom, and a living room. To Sky's surprise, all the rooms were curved, without any corners!

Mac was in the living room, unpacking a big cardboard box.

"This is the new bulb for the lighthouse lamp," Skipper told Sky.

"The old one will need to be replaced soon."

Sky watched Mac lift the huge glass bulb out of the box. "It's very big," she mewed. It was about the size of Joe's soccer ball. Sky could see her reflection in the glass. It was stretched into a funny shape, so that her face looked really wide and her legs looked long and skinny.

"It has to be big," Skipper woofed, "so that the fishermen can see it when they're out at sea. When they see the flashing light, they know they shouldn't get too close. They can keep away from the rocks, and sail safely into the harbor."

"Oh!" Sky mewed. "So that's what the lighthouse is for!"

Skipper wagged his tail proudly. "Do you want to come up and see where the lightbulb goes?" he asked.

"Yes, please," meowed Sky.

Skipper led the way over to the staircase. Sky stopped at the bottom, feeling a little worried. "Do we have to go all the way up *there*?" she asked. Just looking at the steps made her dizzy.

"Yes, right to the top!" Skipper barked, turning around and giving her a friendly lick. "Come on up."

He trotted up the stairs, and Sky followed him. They climbed higher and higher and higher. It was a *very* long way. Soon, Sky was out of breath and her legs were aching.

"Keep going!" Skipper woofed. "It's not far now."

Sky began to feel very hot. Maybe they were climbing all the way up to the sun!

Just when Sky thought she couldn't climb another step, Skipper turned to her. "Here we are," he announced.

They had reached the top of the tower! At first Sky couldn't see anything because it was so bright. Sunshine was streaming in through huge glass windows all around the tower.

Sky blinked. Now she could see the deep blue sea stretching off into the distance.

"Isn't it amazing?" Skipper woofed, his tail wagging madly.

Sky pressed her pink nose against the window. She looked out at the endless, shining waves. "Oh, I really wish I could go out to sea!" she mewed softly.

Skipper stopped wagging his tail. Had Sky said that she wanted to go out to sea? No, he must have heard that wrong. Cats didn't like water! "What did you say?" he woofed.

Sky turned to the puppy. "I want to go out on the fishing boat with Joe's dad," she told him. "But every time I get on the boat, he takes me off again."

Skipper's ears went down. "I wouldn't like to go on a boat," he whimpered. "I like being on dry land!"

Sky didn't seem to hear him. She had pressed her nose to the window again. "Look, Skipper," she mewed. "The fishing boats are coming back."

Skipper and Sky watched the boats

chugging over the water. They looked tiny from high up in the lighthouse. Sky suddenly felt very hungry as she thought about all of the fish they would be bringing back.

"I have to go and help Joe's dad," Sky mewed to Skipper. "Thank you for showing me the lighthouse. 'Bye!" And she ran off down the stairs.

"Sky! Wait!" Skipper barked.

Sky stopped on the lighthouse steps. "What's the matter?"

"Can I come with you?" Skipper woofed. "I'd love to watch the boats come in."

"Sure!" Sky purred.

Together they rushed along the cliff

path. Just as they reached the harbor, Sky stopped. Joe was on the jetty, climbing down the ladder to his little rowboat. He was carrying his fishing rod and a backpack. *He must be going fishing*, Sky thought.

Sky suddenly felt very excited. A very daring idea had popped into her head. "Oh!" she mewed, opening her eyes very wide. "This is my chance to go out to sea!"

Skipper turned around. His big brown eyes looked worried. "Are you *sure* you want to go out to sea?" he asked. "What if you fall out of the boat? Cats aren't supposed to like water. They belong on dry land."

"I'll be fine," Sky told him. "Joe will look after me. See you later!"

Sky ran over to the boat. She was about to call out to Joe, but then she stopped. *Maybe it's better if I hide*, she mewed to herself. *Joe might not let me go otherwise.*

Just then, Joe turned away to untie the boat. Sky saw her chance. She jumped lightly off the jetty and landed in the boat. Quickly, she squeezed under the wooden bench. She peeked out and saw Joe sit down and pick up the oars. Then the boat began to move.

Sky felt very excited. She was on the water at last!

Skipper was standing by the harbor. He saw Sky jump into the boat and hide.

Then he watched Joe row the boat away from the jetty.

Sky's so brave! Skipper woofed to himself. *Maybe cats* can *go out to sea after all. . . .*

chapter four

"Hello, Joe!" Sky purred. She crawled out from under the bench and jumped onto Joe's knee. She had stayed hidden until the boat was far out to sea. She didn't want Joe to take her back home!

Joe's eyes opened wide. "Sky!" he gasped. "What are *you* doing here?"

"I'm going fishing with you," Sky mewed. "I told you I wanted to go out to sea!"

Joe shook his head. "You must really want to go out on a boat," he said, stroking Sky's fur. "Well, I can't take you back now. Just make sure you don't fall in!" He began to row again.

Sky sat on the bench next to Joe, feeling very happy. This was as much fun as she had imagined! She loved the way they bobbed up and down on the waves. She loved hearing the water slap against the sides of the boat. Sky licked her salty whiskers. *It would have been even better if Skipper had come too*, she thought. She turned and looked back at the lighthouse. It was getting smaller and smaller as Joe rowed on.

Soon, Joe stopped and tied the boat to a bright yellow buoy floating on the water. Then he picked up his fishing rod.

Sky stretched out her front paws in delight. "Fish for lunch," she mewed. "Yum!" She curled up on the bench and yawned, feeling warm and sleepy. Purring happily, she closed her eyes. . . .

Back at the lighthouse, Skipper was lying in front of the fire in the living room. He couldn't wait for Sky to come back. He wanted to hear all about her adventure! Skipper yawned and rested his nose on his paws for a snooze.

He woke up with a jump when Mac hurried into the room. He looked worried. Skipper sat up and pricked his ears.

"The lighthouse bulb isn't working," Mac said.

"Oh, no!" Skipper whimpered. His ears went flat and his tail drooped. "We need to replace it before it gets dark."

"We have to get the new bulb in quickly," Mac went on. He shook his head, frowning. "It's very foggy out there, and the boats won't be able to see where the rocks are."

"Foggy?" Skippy barked, puzzled. It

hadn't been foggy when he watched Sky get into Joe's boat.

He trotted out of the lighthouse and stood at the top of the steps. Mac was right, it was *very* foggy. Thick, damp clouds swirled around Skipper, making his fur cold and wet. He could hardly see the

bottom of the steps, let alone the beach or the village by the harbor.

Suddenly, Skipper began to feel very worried about Sky. Had she and Joe come back yet? Or were they still out at sea, lost in this thick, white fog?

chapter five

Sky was eating a very tasty fish. It was the biggest fish she'd ever seen. It was almost as big as she was! "Thank you for catching this fish for me, Joe," she purred.

But something very strange was happening. The more Sky ate, the bigger the fish seemed to get. She tried to push the fish away, but it flapped against her fur, cold and wet and heavy. . . .

Sky sat up with a jump. She hadn't been eating a fish at all. She'd been dreaming. But her fur *was* cold and wet. Sky looked around, her green eyes wide with alarm. The boat was surrounded by thick, white fog. It looked as if they were floating in the middle of a cloud.

"Where's the sea?" Sky wailed. She jumped to her paws and peered over the edge of the boat at the gloomy gray water. She could see the buoy that the boat was tied to. But she couldn't see anything else through the fog. How were they going to find their way home?

Sky looked down at Joe, who had fallen asleep in the bottom of the boat. "Wake up, Joe," she mewed, patting his face with her paw.

Joe opened his eyes and sat up. "It's so foggy!" he gasped. "Don't worry, Sky," he said, stroking the kitten's head. "The lighthouse will help us get home. We will be able to find the harbor once we get past the lighthouse and the rocks."

Sky cheered up. Of course! That was what the lighthouse was for. She looked around, trying to spot the light shining through the fog. But she couldn't see anything.

"That's funny," Joe said. "I can't see the light." He sounded worried. "We'd better try and row back to the shore anyway."

Sky was even more scared now. She was cold and hungry and she wanted to go home. She watched as Joe untied the boat and picked up the oars. How would Joe know which way to go? Where was the light?

Sky crept over and curled up on the bench next to Joe. The heavy blanket of fog made everything very quiet and spooky. She wished she were at home, sitting in front of the fire. Skipper was right. Cats belong on dry land! "I want to go home," she whimpered.

Joe looked a little scared, but he started rowing.

Suddenly, Sky's ears pricked up. She could hear something.

There it was again, louder this time. A long, howling cry, as if someone was calling to them through the fog . . .

chapter six

"Sky!" Skipper howled as loudly as he could from the rocks by the lighthouse. "Sky, where are you-oooo?" He turned his head to one side and listened hard, but he couldn't hear anything.

He tried again. "Sky, where are you-oooo?"

This time Skipper's ears pricked up. Somewhere in the fog he could hear a boy's voice shouting. He carefully padded forward on the slippery rocks. "Joe! Sky!" he barked. "Is that you?"

Out in the boat, Sky could hardly believe her ears. It was Skipper!

"Skipper!" she mewed as loudly as she could. "Where are you?"

"I'm over here," Skipper woofed. "On the rocks near the lighthouse. The bulb isn't working. Mac is trying to replace it with the new one."

So that *was why they couldn't see the lighthouse*, Sky thought.

"Hey! I think I hear a dog," said Joe, sounding surprised. He put down the oars to listen.

Sky mewed eagerly to try and make Joe understand. Skipper was trying to help!

"Could it be Mac's puppy?" Joe asked. The barking got louder.

"If Skipper is standing on the rocks, that

means the lighthouse is over there. So we need to go *this* way. Away from the rocks." He picked up the oars again and began to row.

"Keep barking, Skipper," Sky called. "You're helping us!"

Skipper was puzzled. He couldn't see his friend, he could only hear her. But if he could hear a kitten, that meant she was really close to the rocks. He barked louder.

"Just keep barking," Sky mewed, as Joe steered the boat the other way.

Suddenly, a bright light burst through the fog, sending a shining yellow beam into the sky.

"Look!" Sky mewed. "The lighthouse is working again!"

"Hooray!" Skipper woofed. He was so excited, he almost fell off the rock he was standing on. "Good job, Mac!"

"Now I know we're definitely going in the right direction," said Joe, although he was frightened when he saw how close to the rocks they were. "Don't worry, Sky. We'll be home very soon." He began to row as fast as he could.

Sky stood at the front of the boat and

peered into the fog. She could just make out the harbor and the jetty ahead of them.

"Are you still there, Sky?" woofed Skipper from the rocks.

"We're almost at the jetty," Sky mewed back. She could still hear Skipper as Joe rowed past the lighthouse.

Skipper jumped down from the rocks just as Mac came out of the lighthouse. "Skipper, where are you?" he called. "I've replaced the bulb."

"I need to make sure Sky is OK!" Skipper barked. He raced across the cliffs toward the harbor.

"Skipper, come back!" Mac called. "You might get lost in the fog."

But Skipper didn't stop. He had to go and find Sky!

Sky purred loudly as she saw the jetty loom out of the fog. "We're home, Joe," she meowed in delight. As the boat moved closer to the jetty, Sky saw a small brown shape waiting for them. "It's Skipper!" she mewed.

Skipper ran anxiously up and down the jetty, watching the boat. Then he heard some people running behind him. He looked around. It was Mac, with Joe's dad.

"Joe!" Mr. Kirby called. He looked upset. "Your mom and I were getting very worried about you. You know you're not supposed to go out in the boat on your own!"

"Sorry, Dad," said Joe. "I just wanted to go fishing." He reached out and grabbed the side of the jetty to pull the boat closer. Then he tied up the boat and lifted Sky onto the jetty.

She ran over to Skipper and rubbed her head against the puppy's warm, furry shoulder. "Oh, Skipper! I am so glad to see you!"

Skipper gave Sky a big lick on her pink nose.

Joe's dad saw the kitten, and looked very surprised. "What is Sky doing here?"

"She came fishing with me!" Joe said. "It was fun at first. But then we got lost when the fog rolled in."

"How did you find your way back?" asked Mr. Kirby.

"Oh, that was easy," Sky purred. "It was all thanks to Skipper!"

"The lighthouse wasn't working," Joe said. "Luckily, Skipper was out on the rocks. I could hear him barking, so I knew which way to go."

Mac smiled and patted Skipper's head. "Great job, Skipper," he said. "That's just what a lighthouse puppy should do!"

"You're a hero," mewed Sky.

The puppy looked very pleased. "I am?" he woofed.

"Yes," purred Sky. "You're the best lighthouse puppy in the whole world!"

The next day, the fog had lifted and it was sunny and warm. Skipper and Sky sat by the harbor, watching the fishermen get ready to go out in the boats.

Skipper had something very important to show Sky. "Look at my medal," he woofed proudly. "Mac gave it to me this morning."

Sky admired the gold medal on Skipper's collar. "It's very shiny," she mewed.

"It says that I'm the *Official Lighthouse Puppy*," Skipper explained, wagging his tail.

"I'm glad you got a medal," Sky purred. "You helped me *twice* yesterday. First when I was stuck in the net, then when Joe and I got lost in the fog. You're my best friend, Skipper!"

"And you're *my* best friend," Skipper woofed.

The fishermen were ready to go now. Joe's dad jumped on board the *Jolly Jack* with a cheerful wave.

Skipper and Sky watched as the boats began to chug out of the harbor. "Don't you want to go out to sea today?" Skipper asked.

Sky looked around the harbor. Joe was

sitting on the wall, waving to his dad and eating an ice cream cone. The sun was hot on Sky's fur, and her tummy was full. She'd had fish for breakfast, and there would be more fresh fish to eat when the boats came back.

"Why would I want to go out to sea?" she mewed at last. "I like dry land best!"